Jeremiah Learns to Read

Jo Ellen Bogart

Laura Fernandez & Rick Jacobson

SCHOLASTIC CANADA LTD.

The paintings for this book were done in oil on canvas.
A special thank you to John and Henriette Ford, the models for Jeremiah and Juliana.

This book was designed in QuarkXPress,
with type set in 18 pt Esprit Medium.

Scholastic Canada Ltd.
175 Hillmount Road, Markham, Ontario L6C 1Z7

Scholastic Inc.
555 Broadway, New York, NY 10012, USA

Scholastic Australia Pty Limited
PO Box 579, Gosford, NSW 2250, Australia

Scholastic New Zealand Limited
Private Bag 94407, Greenmount, Auckland, New Zealand

Scholastic Ltd.
Villiers House, Clarendon Avenue, Leamington Spa,
Warwickshire CV32 5PR, UK

Canadian Cataloguing in Publication Data

Bogart, Jo Ellen, 1945-
Jeremiah learns to read

ISBN 0-590-51527-6

I. Fernandez, Laura. II. Jacobson, Rick. III. Title.

PS8553.O465J47 1999   jC813'.54   C99-930533-6

8 7 6 5 4 3 2 1   Printed and Bound in Canada   9 /9 0 1 2 3 4 /0

For those who are learning the joys of reading.
—J.E.B

This book is dedicated to those, young and old, who are learning to read,
including our children Michael, Maite and Mercedes.
A wonderful world will open up to you!
—L.F. & R.J.

Jeremiah knew how to build a split-rail fence
and he knew how to cook buttermilk pancakes,
but he didn't know how to read.

2

Jeremiah knew how to make a table out of a tree, or sweet syrup from its sap, but he didn't know how to read.

Jeremiah knew how to grow beautiful tomatoes,
long green cucumbers and juicy cobs of corn, but
he didn't know how to read.

He knew the tracks of the animals and the signs
of the seasons, but he didn't know the letters and
the words.

"I want to learn to read," he said to his brother Jackson.

"You're an old man, Jeremiah," said Jackson. "You have children and grandchildren and you can do almost anything."

"But I can't read," said Jeremiah.

"Fine," said his brother. "Then learn."

"I want to learn to read," Jeremiah said to his wife, Juliana.

"You're wonderful just the way you are," said Juliana, and she stroked his grey beard.

"But I can be even better," he said.

"Fine," said his wife. "Learn. Then you can read to me." She smiled at him over her knitting.

"I want to learn to read," Jeremiah said to his old sheepdog. The old sheepdog just looked at him, then lay down on the rag rug by Jeremiah's feet.

Jeremiah thought, "How can I learn to read? My brother can't teach me. My wife can't teach me. This old dog can't teach me. How will I learn?"

Jeremiah thought and thought, and then he smiled.

The next morning, Jeremiah got up at sunrise and did his chores. Then he washed his face and his hands, brushed his hair and his beard, and put on his favourite shirt. He made biscuits and gravy and sliced tomatoes for breakfast, and packed a sandwich for his lunch. Then he kissed Juliana goodbye and walked out the door.

He joined a group of children
walking down the tree-shaded lane.
When they went into the schoolhouse,
Jeremiah went in, too. Mrs. Trumble
smiled when she saw him.

"I want to learn to read," he told
her. She pointed toward an empty seat
and Jeremiah sat down.

"Class," said Mrs. Trumble, "we
have a new student today."

Jeremiah started by learning the letters and the sounds they made. Some of the children helped him. At recess, he sat under a tree and told stories. He showed Sarah and David how to chirp like a chickadee and honk like a goose.

Soon Jeremiah was learning words.
He studied his lessons carefully. He
practised his writing every day.

Jeremiah loved it when the teacher
and the older children read to the class.
Sometimes he drew pictures while
he listened.

Jeremiah was learning, but he was teaching, too. He showed the Miller twins how to whittle with a pocketknife. He taught Mrs. Trumble how to make applesauce and how to whistle through her teeth.

After a while, Jeremiah was putting words together and writing his own stories. He wrote about saving a baby squirrel. He wrote about swimming in the river. He wrote about the day he met his wife.

Juliana watched Jeremiah practising his writing on the table after supper. "When are you going to read to me?" she asked.

"When the time is right," he answered.

One day, Jeremiah took a book
of poems home from school.
The poems were about trees and
clouds and streams and swiftly
running deer. Jeremiah hid it
under his pillow. That night,
when he and Juliana went to bed,
he pulled out the book.

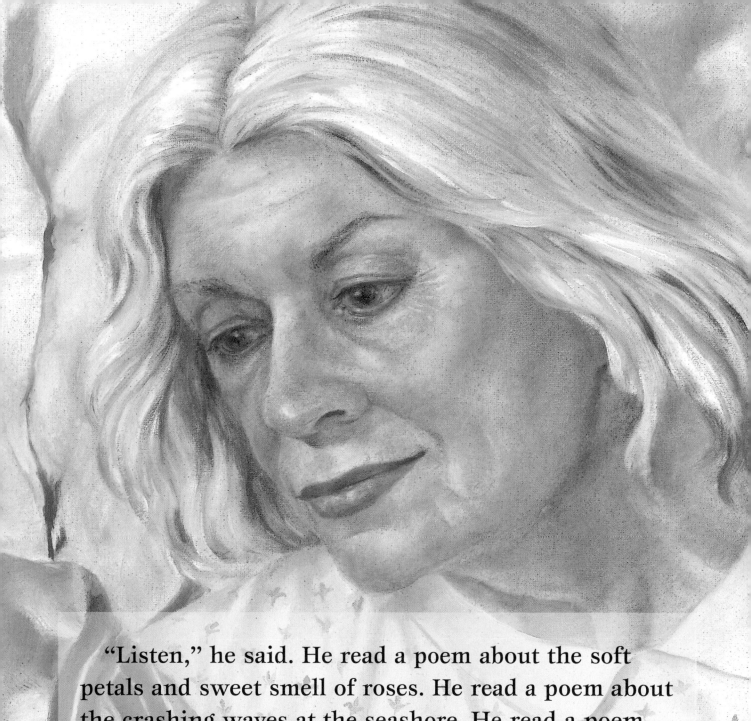

"Listen," he said. He read a poem about the soft petals and sweet smell of roses. He read a poem about the crashing waves at the seashore. He read a poem about love.

Juliana looked into her husband's grey eyes. "Oh, Jeremiah," she said. "I want to learn to read."

Jeremiah smiled at Juliana. "First thing after breakfast, my love." And Jeremiah turned off the light.